# Little Alf the Ma

# By Hannah Russell

# Little Alf the Magic Helper

## (The Christmas sequel)

Believe in Magic and you will find it...

\*\*\*

It has been nearly one whole year since Hannah first found Little Alf in the Magical Forest...

This year was their first Christmas together at Meadowlea Stables, and Hannah couldn't be happier.

Hannah had previously discovered the magic of Little Alf when they were in the forest together one day and had stumbled across an ancient oak tree which was no ordinary tree.

One adventure in the local library led Hannah to discover an old book which changed her life forever. She had found the ultimate key to everyone's dreams.

When Hannah and Little Alf enter the magic forest and whisper the words next to the mysterious tree...

'Believe in magic and you will find it'

...a magical transformation takes place which means Little Alf is able to talk to Hannah...

\*\*\*

# Chapter 1

Finally the Christmas tree had been decorated.

The tree was as tall as the living room and almost as wide as the bay windows it stood in, blocking out the view of the North Yorkshire Dales from Hannah's living room window.

Its needles were thick and glossy and filled the room with a delicious piney smell. The bottom of the tree was covered in white snow and red baubles but the top shined and twinkled as the light came through.

'Here's another bauble' Hannah's Mum said as she passed it to her.

Hannah studied the bauble delicately; its red paint had slightly chipped around the edge of the wooden rocking horse, but you could still see the beautiful handcraft and detail someone had in making it.

'Every bauble has its own story' Hannah thought to herself as she placed it on the tree and stood back to admire the decorations as they twinkled and shined.

'You've forgotten something' Hannah's Dad said as he pulled a box of green, red and white-striped candy canes from behind his back.

'How could I forget!' Hannah said, giggling as she smelt the tasty peppermint.

She finished decorating the tree with her brother John and stood and admired it once again.

'Wow,that looks fantastic!' Hannah's Mum said as she set down a tray with four steaming hot chocolates topped with whipped cream and fluffy marshmallows.

'Mum, can I go to the stables now the tree is decorated?' Hannah asked hopefully as she sipped her hot chocolate.

'Well I was just going to make a batch of mince pies but I suppose I could drop you off first' said Mum.

'I think it might snow later, Hannah, so you best wrap up warm' said Hannah's Dad as he looked outside.

'I will, don't worry!' Hannah shouted as she leapt up the stairs to get changed into her riding gear. She was so excited, she loved going to the stables to see Little Alf.

Little Alf was Hannah's miniature Shetland pony. She had found him last year in the Magical Forest. He had been completely wild when Hannah found him but they had instantly bonded and ever since then Little Alf and Hannah have never been found far apart. Recently they embarked on a magical adventure into the mysterious forest, where Hannah found out about a very special secret that Little Alf held...

***

Hannah jumped out of the car with her yellow wellies on as soon as her Mum pulled the car into Meadowlea Stables.

'Bye Mum, see you later' Hannah shouted as she ran down the yard.

'Hannah, be careful its icy today!'

'Ooooft!' Hannah cried, as she landed on the ground.

'I did warn you it was icy today and you raced into the yard rather fast! It's winter so you have to be extra careful' Ruth said, chuckling as she helped Hannah to her feet.

'Whoops! I'm just so excited to see Little Alf this morning' Hannah giggled, brushing the ice off her jodhpurs.

'I know you are! You are every day! Just be careful outside the barn, it's very icy outside the entrance' Ruth warned Hannah.

'Okay' Hannah said happily as she gingerly tiptoed across the ice patches towards the barn.

As she opened the wooden barn door she heard the whinny from Little Alf's stable...

Approaching, she could hear Little Alf snorting and stamping his feet, waiting to see her.

'Hello Alf' Hannah beamed as he snorted and shook his head before nuzzling her pocket.

'Okay, okay you can have a carrot' Hannah giggled as Little Alf pulled at her pockets.

'Hi Hannah! I think it's going to snow today' Tilly shouted as she bounded into the barn with Jack, her black and white cob.

'My Dad said that too this morning! Wouldn't it be nice if we had snow for Christmas?' Hannah said excitedly!

'That would be magical!' Tilly giggled as she led Jack into his stable and began to untack him.

'Although I'm not sure what the horses would think to it' Hannah said as she patted Alfie.

'Last year when it snowed Jack loved it! He was rolling around in it for ages, although he got rather wet and cold once he'd finished playing' Tilly replied.

'Hmmm, maybe it wouldn't be so good then. Alfie doesn't like getting cold' said Hannah, buckling up Alfie's headcollar.

She walked out of the barn with a spring in her step and Little Alf by her side. He swished his head and snorted as he began to trot up the lane excitedly. He knew exactly where they were going and Hannah began to feel the magical feeling in her stomach as they headed towards the enchanted forest...

# Chapter 2

Hannah tiptoed around the frozen puddles and headed towards the old wooden oak bridge. The bridge had a slight glimmer of crystal blue from the frost the previous evening. As the sun shone onto the bridge, Hannah could see the long glittering icicles dangling along the bottom of the oak bridge.

She gently stepped onto the bridge with Little Alf by her side and took one foot forward, trying to avoid the ice on the ground below. She slipped and quickly grabbed the bridge rail to stop her from falling over.

'I don't think my yellow wellies have much grip, Alf' Hannah chuckled as she rebalanced herself and carried on until they reached the other side. Alfie jumped and snorted at the nearby tree as a rabbit popped out and ran up the track towards the Magical

Forest... Although the day was cold, the forest was bright and the branches swayed with the light breeze which skimmed through the trees, showing the twinkle of the branches as the ice clung to the dying winter leaves. Little Alf began to swish his tail and pull towards the forest as they got deeper into the trees.

'Alright, Alf! We are going, don't worry' Hannah giggled as Alfie shook his head and snorted, grabbing an orange rusted leaf from the woodland floor.

'You're so cheeky!' Hannah said, patting him.

As they wandered deeper in the forest, Hannah could feel the magic building up and she couldn't wait to get to the oak tree once again. She loved being able to talk to Little Alf and knew she was extremely lucky that she could. She had often heard people saying at the stables how they would love to be able to talk to their horses.

Hannah sometimes wished she could tell her parents about being able to talk to Little Alf, but knew she couldn't as they would never believe her and it could ruin the bond she had with him...

The oak tree was now in sight and as they drew nearer Hannah could see the small twinkles beginning to form around the bottom of the tree as they glistened off the bark. They had now picked up speed to a slow jog, and Alfie was bounding towards the tree with excitement. Once they reached the tree Hannah whispered the words...

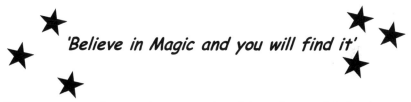

*'Believe in Magic and you will find it'*

There was a huge shower of golden dust which shot up from the tree and surrounded Alfie and Hannah, nearly knocking them both over. The golden dust once again glittered like stars and danced like waves on the sea. It always amazed Hannah, no matter how many times she came to the oak tree, how pretty the dust was and how the magic always worked.

The branches twinkled as the leaves began to change colour into emerald greens and icy blues; each season the leaves had changed to a different colour when Hannah whispered the magic words. Once the dust had settled and the tree was gently swaying and twinkling with the breeze, Hannah gently sat down on the grass underneath the tree.

'Alfie' Hannah whispered, 'Alfie'.


*'Hello Hannah'*


Hannah giggled and patted Little Alf. She loved hearing his voice and she still hadn't got used to the magic feeling she felt when he talked.

'Alfie, I'm so glad I have you! I'm so excited for Christmas. Just one week until Santa comes to visit!'


*'I wonder what he will bring me. I have been a very good pony this year'*


This made Hannah giggle 'You have been a very cheeky pony this year! Santa is coming to Leyburn tomorrow night to switch on the Christmas tree lights! I am so excited'


*'Can I come?'*

'Alfie I don't think I could explain that one to Mum and Dad! Although you probably would fit in the car!' Hannah said, laughing.

There was suddenly a loud bang from the forest and the clatter of something moving fast. The tree began to sway and change back to its usual form; Alfie snorted and shook his head as the dust began to fade away. Hannah began to panic... what was in the forest?

A sudden loud rippling sound began ringing through the trees; Hannah had never heard anything like it before. Alfie began to pull towards the stables and Hannah knew he could no longer talk to her as the magic had worn off with the sound of an intruder....

Alfie had now taken flight; Hannah was struggling to hold him as he tugged and pulled her towards the stables, the loud noise was beginning to get nearer and the bushes were beginning to rustle. Hannah was desperate to know where the noise was coming from, but knew Alfie was right - they had to get away, and fast...

She began to run, with Little Alf storming ahead, she slipped on the mud and icy surface below, her yellow wellies now covered in mud. They heard the noise again, loud and clear this time, it sounded like an animal - but what animal could make that sound? There certainly weren't any bears in the Yorkshire Dales!

Hannah was beginning to slow down as she became tired, but Alfie was still trying to pull her out of the forest. She began to pick up her pace again, and had finally reached the wooden bridge which led into the forest. Alfie was not walking calmly as they reached the bridge. Hannah looked around to see if the creature had followed her, but all she could see was the trees gently swaying, everything seemed as it usually was.

'So strange' Hannah whispered, confused as she looked down at her trousers which were now covered in mud, her yellow wellies the colour of the old oak bridge. Little Alf licked Hannah's hand and nudged her pocket.

'Okay, you can have a carrot, just don't tell anyone' Hannah said as she patted his mane.

'I'm sorry we couldn't talk for longer, Alfie. Whatever is in that wood isn't very happy at all. Thank you for getting me out of there' she sighed as Alfie rested his head against her knee.

They gingerly headed back over the bridge towards the stables and all Hannah could think about was what was lurking in the forest and whether it was safe? She knew she had to tell Ruth, as this could put the other riders in serious danger...

***

Back at the stables, Hannah put Little Alf back and headed off to find Ruth, but as she got into the yard she saw there were two police cars and another unusual car in the yard, which was very strange as usually people were only allowed to park in the car park.

Hannah suddenly began to panic and hurried into the office. She quickly opened the door and was met by Ruth, who was sitting down on the sofa opposite the policeman.

'What's happened?' Hannah asked, worriedly.

Ruth sighed 'Hannah can you please go sit in the kitchen with the rest of the group, make yourself a drink and sit with them. I will come and talk to you all soon'.

'I have something to tell you about the forest though, I'm worried it might be dangerous' Hannah spluttered. The Police Officers turned around and looked at her. Hannah gulped.

'You've been to the forest this morning?' Ruth asked, looking concerned.

'Of course I have! I go every weekend! I did tell you I was going' Hannah said, smiling as she thought about her previous trips to the forest.

'You'd best sit down, we might want to ask you some questions' said the Police Officer with the wavy brown hair.

'Okay...' Hannah said, flashing a quick glance at Ruth.

'We've had several reports this morning about an unusual sighting and noises coming from the forest, so we have come up here to warn everybody to stay away from there until further notice whilst an investigation takes place.' The Police Officer said as he looked at Hannah.

'So we can't go in the forest again?' Hannah said, wondering how she would be able to talk to Alfie now.

She suddenly began to get very worried; she couldn't imagine not being able to talk to him.

'We're not saying forever, but it is best that nobody goes out riding until more investigations have been done. Now can you tell me what you heard or saw this morning?' the officer asked as he brought out a small pad of paper and a pen.

'Ermm well... I didn't see anything but I heard a loud noise; it was like something unhappy, like it was angry, it was screeching through the forest almost like an animal maybe..'

'Hmmmmm' the officer said as he quickly jotted down some notes.

'So you never saw this creature?' he asked.

'No, but my pony might have done... I could ask...' Hannah quickly had to stop herself. Of course she couldn't tell them she could ask Little Alf, as nobody knew that he could talk, and they wouldn't believe her anyway. The officer stared at her suspiciously.

'Right that will be all Hannah, you may go' the officer said as he shut his notepad. Hannah swiftly jumped off the sofa and ran around towards the stables kitchen, where she was suddenly hit with the strong smell of gingerbread.

'Hannah, you're back! I'm so happy! There's a policeman talking to Ruth in the office; we were so worried' Tilly said as she leapt towards Hannah and hugged her.

'Would you like a gingerbread hot chocolate Hannah? You look like you need warming up!' Stacey, one of the stable girls, asked.

'Y...eee...sss ple...ease... Hannah stuttered.

'What's the matter Hannah?' Tilly asked worriedly.

'Can we all sit down please girls!' Ruth bellowed as she walked into the kitchen. Hannah let out a huge sigh of relief that she didn't have to explain to the group why the Police had arrived.

'Right team, as you all saw earlier, the Police have paid us a visit this morning'. Some of the group gasped at the news; obviously not everyone knew they had been.

'Well they have been today to inform us that there is a wild creature in the forest, and it's suspected to be dangerous due to an incident last night. The creature broke in to Colliwath Stables which is owned by Rusty, the lady who retrains ex-racehorses.

The creature appears to have made large holes in the stable doors, and also broke into the feed room and ate the supply of carrots. The horses were unharmed but very unsettled this morning. The Police have been to tell us that the forest is not allowed to be used until they tell us otherwise. They've also told us we should not go out riding until there's more information.'

There were loud gasps from around the room, which soon broke into chaos with people talking over each other.

'Quieten down please, team!' Ruth shouted.

'If you don't own a horse here at the stables but were having a riding lesson this afternoon, I have rung your parents and told them to come pick you up after dinner. For those of you who have a horse here at the stable you are only allowed to remain on the premises, and we have been told to keep the horses indoors to be 100% safe and secure. I'm sure the problem will soon be solved'

Silence fell around the room; everyone was shocked and Hannah was devastated. It was only a week until Christmas, and she wouldn't be able to spend her Christmas break with Alfie, as she knew her parents wouldn't let her go to the stables alone now. She knew she could help solve the problem, but that would mean going back into the forest....

# Chapter 3

When everybody who didn't own a horse at the stables had gone home, Hannah headed outside to visit Alfie. It had now begun to snow outside and it was soon settling on the ground.

'I think I'll give your parents a call Hannah. If it snows anymore you'll be trapped here overnight!' Ruth said.

'Really?' Hannah beamed.

Ruth laughed, 'I know you would live in Alfie's stable if you could, but it is very cold at night and you're not built like a horse'.

Hannah sighed. She would love for Alfie to be able to live in her bedroom, especially tonight as she was so worried about the creature in the forest. She headed down to the stables as the snow began to flutter around her. The sky was now covered with white fluffy clouds and the light was beginning to fade. Hannah loved Christmas, but hated how the nights soon became very dark, she slowly pulled the barn door open and went inside to Little Alf's stable.

As she walked down to the barn all the horses stuck their heads over the doors and greeted her. Paddy, the black and white gypsy cob Hannah usually rode, whinnied loudly as she got near him.

'Hello Paddy' Hannah laughed as she tickled his nose. He pricked his ears forward and held his nose up to her head,before blowing softly. Hannah shrieked as he tickled her face.

She gently crept down to the next stable to see that Badger, the black and white Welsh Section C, was softly sleeping in the corner of his bed. Hannah first rode Badger when she came to the stables, but since then Ruth had decided to retire him, as he was now twenty-two years old and used to help settle young horses in their paddocks.

Hannah smiled to herself as she peered over to see Pepper, the stable's miniature Shetland, also fast asleep in the corner of his bed. Hannah loved Pepper; he sometimes went in the same paddock as Alfie and they would play together all day. As she carried along down the barn she was soon outside Alfie's stable and stopped to gently unbolt the door. Alfie was standing waiting for her.

'Alfie!' Hannah beamed as she slid down against the stable door to sit on the straw beneath her. Alfie stepped forward and she brushed his mane away so she could tickle his forehead. He nuzzled her as she stroked him.

'What are we going to do, Alfie? Ruth will never let us in the forest now' Hannah sighed. Alfie squealed and stamped his feet.

'Oh I wish I could talk to you all the time What if they never find the creature and we can't go in ever again...?' Alfie stamped his feet again and nudged her.

'I wouldn't ever let that happen, would I!' Hannah giggled as she patted him.

'Hannah, your parents are here!' she heard Ruth shout. She opened the stable door and Alfie tried to escape and barge through the door too.

'NO Alfie you can't come out too, it isn't safe outside' Alfie snorted and let out a huge whinny as he kicked the stable door.

'What's the matter?' Hannah asked, confused.

Alfie kicked the door again and snorted, this time letting out an even louder whinny.

'What's up with the little fella?' Hannah's Dad asked as he came through the barn door.

'I don't know, he doesn't seem very happy' Hannah said, panicking.

'Probably just the eventful day you've had today. Ruth's just filled me in; maybe it's unsettled him' her Dad replied.

'Can we stay just a little longer please, to make sure he's okay?' Hannah asked.

'As much as I would love to say yes, we can't Hannah, because we have to join in with the Christmas carols tonight, and I told your brother we'd pick him up from football. Alfie will be okay, don't worry, he has his warm bed. Plus if it snows any more we might get stuck in the snow'.

Hannah sighed and looked at Little Alf one last time before heading outside towards the car. She knew Little Alf had been trying to tell her something, but what could it be...?

***

The village had all braved the frosty weather and were wrapped up warm ready to sing at the Christmas Festival. The snow had eventually stopped and the sky was now clear with just the twinkly stars shining. Hannah was just wondering what Little Alf was doing when a snowball landed next to her foot!

'Oy! Who was that?' Hannah cried.

'Whoops, sorry! I was aiming for Dad', Hannah's brother John said.

'I bet you weren't!' Hannah said, laughing.

'Right come on everyone, the first song is about to start' a voice bellowed out. Hannah went to stand next to her family as the village Christmas lights were turned on. She was so excited as the music started and they began to sing the first Christmas song... 'Jingle bells... Jingle bells... '.

By the time the Christmas songs had finished and everybody had sipped their hot drinks and munched their mince pies, Hannah was yawning.

'I think it's time we went home' Hannah's Mum said.

'Me too' said her Dad.

They wandered up the village and headed back towards home. As Hannah got into her bed, all she could think about was the forest, and how she would ever be able to talk to Little Alf.

# Chapter 4

Hannah jumped out of her bed the next day and threw back her curtains to see that the snow had started to fall again and was swirling softly to the

ground. A pure white sheet had settled on the ground overnight and was delicately glistering and twinkling as the sun shone down. The branches were laced with crystal icicles and the floor was frozen as it sparkled in the sun. Hannah ran downstairs and grabbed her yellow wellies and woolly hat, before running outside into the fresh snow. As she stepped outside she could hear children playing down the street and the dog barking at them from across the road.

'I'd best try dig the car out!' Hannah's Dad said, as he stepped outside with his hat and gloves on.

'Do you think we'll make it to the stables today?' Hannah asked hopefully.

'If it doesn't snow any more we should be able to make it there' he replied.

Hannah let out a huge sigh of relief as she shivered in the morning breeze.

'Why don't you get your breakfast? Then we should be able to go see Alfie'.

'Oh good' Hannah said happily as she skipped inside.

Wandering into the kitchen where she was met with a strong smell of coffee and freshly made pancakes, she looked up to the notice board where her chocolate advent calendar was hanging on the metal hook and gently brought it down to open door number 19. She smiled to herself - just six days until Christmas!

Then she suddenly thought about Little Alf and what might be lurking in the forest. She knew she had to try and get to the oak tree to ask Little Alf about what it could be, but didn't know how she could get there without Ruth realising. She sat down at the table while she watched her Mum make some more pancakes topped with syrup, and began to think about how she could solve the mystery...

'Are you day dreaming, Hannah?'

'No - just thinking, Mum!'

'Did you hear what I asked you?'

'No, sorry Mum' Hannah replied.

'I was just wondering if you wanted a hot chocolate to warm you up before you go outside'.

'Of course I do' Hannah said, giggling.

'I thought you might say that' her Mum replied as she set down a mug of steaming hot chocolate.

***

'I hope it doesn't snow anymore, that was scary' Hannah said as she hopped out of the car.

'Let's hope not. If it starts snowing anymore I'll have to come pick you up early, Hannah' her Dad said.

'Okay, then' Hannah sighed.

She stood and watched as her Dad drove back down the icy lane. Her parents had told her that she was strictly only allowed to stay at Meadowlea Stables today and, with the wild animal still on the loose, was not allowed into the forest.

She wandered around to the old tack room, and pulled the door open. A strong smell of leather greeted her. She loved the tack room. Ruth had told her that it had been around for over 100 years, and used to be an old barn where the sheep would live in the cold winters. The old barn door was now rusted around the edges and the hinges creaked as it opened, but it was one of the remaining features. It was the old door where Hannah had first seen the message 'Believe in magic and you will find it' carved into the structure underneath a very delicate drawing of an oak tree...

*'Believe in Magic and you will find it'*

Hannah gently ran her finger along the lettering and felt a jolt as it sent a wave of magic through her body. She giggled as it tingled her finger; it was something she had become used to over the past few months. Hannah was reaching up to get Alfie's headcollar when she felt a breeze tickle past her, she quickly turned around to see the tack room door had gently swung open...

'That's odd' Hannah thought. She was sure she had shut the door behind her, and it was usually too heavy to swing open anyway...

As she headed towards the door she saw a gentle glow as new words began to form across the structure... Hannah jumped back; she had only ever seen real magic happen next to the oak tree before. She stood and watched as the dust swirled and laced new words together underneath the picture of the oak tree, but this was no ordinary dust - this was silver, red and green which twinkled in the dull room, she gasped as it magically danced before coming to a halt... Hannah saw the new words which had been formed.

*Believe the magic and solve the mystery...*

'Believe the magic and solve the mystery' Hannah whispered to herself. She frowned, confused at what the words might mean.

As she began to think, she saw the silver dust had once again begun to carve into the door, but this time it wasn't words, but a picture. She tilted her head, eager to see what the dust was forming as it spiralled and jumped...

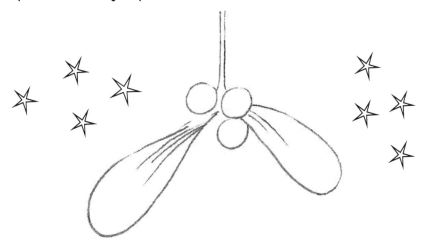

Hannah looked at the drawing, confused, as the last of the silver glittery dust vanished. She studied the diagram as she ran her fingers up and down it, not sure what it was. It almost seemed familiar somehow, as if she had seen the drawing before, but she wasn't sure where. Then she suddenly gasped and stood back to admire the door.

She realised she had seen the drawing before. It was everywhere at the moment! The diagram in front of her was *mistletoe*. She stared at the drawing a while longer before pushing open the heavy creaking door and heading towards the stables kitchen to find Ruth. As she wandered up the yard, all she could think about was how mistletoe could link to the forest and the mysterious creature...

*****

Hi Everyone!

Sorry it is short notice but I have gone Christmas shopping today!

If there is an emergency call, ring my mobile number, I will have it with me all day.

Nobody is to go out of the yard today. If you want to ride your horses go in the ménage!

(Hannah if you want to take Little Alf for a walk just walk him around the yard or let him play with Pepper in the ménage.)

If I find out that anyone has gone into the forest today there will be consequences for your actions.

Have fun!

Ruth

x

P.S. if it snows you are all to ring your parents and be collected! I don't want anyone trapped here overnight! I will be back around 5:00pm.

Hannah read the note once again; she couldn't believe everyone had been left to do what they wanted for the day, and so far she hadn't seen anyone else on the yard! She read the note a third time, wondering what consequences she would face if she tried to go into the forest. Now she had seen the message on the tack room door she knew she had to take Alfie and visit the oak tree with nobody else around. She was sure she could make it there and back before 5:00pm...

***

The snow was soft and untouched as Hannah and Alfie headed towards the forest. Alfie jumped and rolled in the snow, giddily making new tracks and Hannah giggled next to him as she too jumped into fresh patches of snow.

Alfie bounced, squealed and leaped, before storming ahead towards the forest.

'Alfie, wait there' Hannah instructed, as she ran, trying to keep up with him.

He stood and snorted, looking back at Hannah as she struggled through the snow after him. It was deeper as they got nearer to the forest and in places it was spilling over Hannah's yellow wellies. She tried to wiggle her toes as the snow began to melt in her boots, but it was no good, her toes were already beginning to go numb with the chill.

As she reached Alfie she unclipped her rucksack from her back. She had made sure to bring Alfie's rug in case he got cold and extra supplies of carrots for him, with a flask of hot chocolate in case she got cold too.

They had finally reached the edge of the forest, both tired from battling the snow. Hannah glanced back to look at the tracks they had made, hoping that if anyone turned up to the yard they wouldn't realise that she and Alfie were gone.

The sun was beginning to shine around the forest, which twinkled as they headed through the trees, almost welcoming them as the branches weighed down with mounds of snow which was slowly beginning to melt and drop to the floor.

'Ahh!' Hannah screamed as snow slowly slithered down her back. Alfie jumped as Hannah danced around trying to get the cold snow away from her skin.

'Wow that was cold! Sorry, Alf!' she said, giggling as she gave him a carrot to munch. As they slowly ploughed through the snow, the oak tree began to come into sight...As Hannah got nearer to it, she began to feel the magic. Alfie squealed and bucked as they reached the tree.

## 'Believe in magic and you will find it...'

...Hannah whispered. She stood back and waited for the tree to transform... but nothing happened.

## 'Believe in magic and you will find it...'

she whispered again, but still nothing happened.

Hannah looked at Alfie, who also had a puzzled look. She slowly reached out to touch the tree but didn't feel the magic zip through her like she usually did, so she touched the tree with her other hand, but felt nothing.

Alfie began to stamp his feet and get restless as Hannah headed around the tree to investigate. She slowly crept around looking at the tree but it still looked the same, apart from the snow which was gently glistering on top of the branches. The leaves were sparkling in the sun where the ice had clung to the veins of the leaves, and the acorns were still webbed to the tree. Suddenly

Hannah heard a knocking sound and turned around to see that Little Alf was kicking the tree.

'What you doing Alfie?' Hannah asked as she knelt down to look at the tree, slowly lacing her hands along it where Alfie had been kicking, but it still looked the same. She frowned, wondering what Alfie could be trying to tell her.

He tugged at Hannah's coat and began to hoof the floor, so she crawled over and started to sweep away the snow to see what Alfie was showing her, but there was nothing there. She sat back against the oak tree, puzzled at the mystery, and began to think of everything that had happened, from the mysterious creature to the tack room door, but nothing made sense.

Alfie nudged Hannah again and began to pull past the oak tree and stamp on the snow, so she gingerly picked up his leadrope and wandered over to the spot where he was standing. She knelt down and looked at the snow to see it had a small hole in the top layer. She stood up and studied it to see that there were tracks leading deeper into the forest...

Hannah jolted up quickly and stumbled backwards; she had never seen tracks like that before - could this be the link to the mysterious creature?

'Well done, Alfie!' Hannah giggled as she patted him and gave him a carrot. Alfie swished his head and whinnied. Suddenly a huge gust of wind made the oak tree sway and release the snow it held on the branches...

## 'Believe the magic and solve the mystery... '

'Alfie, was that you?' Hannah asked, looking down at him...

# 'Believe the magic and solve the mystery... '

The words whipped past Hannah again, she began to look around but nothing was there...

# 'Believe the magic and solve the mystery... '

This time the words were clearer and echoed gently in the breeze.

'Believe the magic and solve the mystery' Hannah whispered to herself. She looked down at Alfie who was standing patiently looking at her, and she knew she had to follow the tracks deeper into the wood....

# Chapter 5

Hannah and Little Alf began to follow the hoof prints into the forest, the wind rattling through the trees, making the snow sprinkle like dust across the floor, which made it hard to see the tracks, but Hannah was determined to find out what the creature was and why the magic had stopped working. She couldn't think about never being able to talk to Little Alf again. She carried on following the tracks when suddenly they stopped.... She looked left and right, but the tracks were nowhere to be found.

'How strange' Hannah muttered to herself as she carried on looking at the snow on the floor; the hoof prints looked the same, but the very last one was oddly shaped, almost as if the creature had taken off into the sky... but she knew she must be looking at the prints wrongly because a creature this large couldn't fly...

Alfie began to pull forward, taking Hannah with him.

'Where you going, Alfie? The tracks have stopped', but he carried on pulling forward and she knew she had to follow him, as the last time she had doubted him he had been right.

The deeper into the forest they went, the deeper the snow became, and they were both now struggling to walk, and the snow was spilling over Hannah's yellow wellies, sending a shiver down her spine and creating goosebumps on her skin. It wasn't long before her teeth began to chatter as the cold caught her breath.

They both stopped to rest, out of breath from trudging through the snow. Hannah quickly whipped off her rucksack and brought out her flask of steaming hot chocolate. Steadily pouring herself a cup, she clasped the edges as it began to warm up her icy hands which were numb from the cold. She grabbed a carrot for Little Alf and buckled his rug up tighter to keep the warmth from seeping out of his fluffy coat.

As Alfie began to crunch his carrot she felt something move behind her... Alfie pricked his ears and snorted, and she knew that, whatever was behind her, Alfie didn't like the sight of it, as he began to back up further into the snow.

Hannah turned around hesitantly, not sure what was behind her and not wanting to scare the creature. She slowly moved her feet as calmly as possible to get a glimpse, but, as she turned, her foot got caught in her rucksack and she fell to the ground. There was a large snort and a scatter of snow, Hannah quickly opened her eyes and spun round trying to get a glimpse as the creature dashed off through the forest. She jumped up, searching through the trees, but she couldn't see anything.

Alfie was snorting and holding his head high, clearly unsettled by whatever he had just seen, Hannah gently patted him, trying to settle him back down. She slowly crept over to where she had been standing to study the hoof prints, and they were the same ones that she had seen next to the oak tree. Hannah wished the magic was still working, then she would be able to ask Alfie about what he had just witnessed.

They stood there a while longer, as she studied the tracks. Hannah looked at Little Alf who happily had his head buried in her rucksack, munching his way through the carrots. She knew that if she didn't follow the tracks she might never be able to locate the creature again, which would mean she would never be able to talk to Alfie again.... A soft breeze rolled past them sending another shiver down Hannah's spine, reminding her how cold she really was. She looked up at the sky to see that thick white clouds were beginning to form, threatening to snow once again.

'What should we do, Alf?' she sighed as he snatched another carrot from the rucksack. She looked at the tracks one last time before deciding to head back to the stables; she knew if she was out any longer they could be in danger of getting lost in the snow or getting extremely cold. She picked up Alfie's lead rope and began to head back through the trees. Alfie wouldn't move, so she tugged on his lead rope again.

'Come on Alfie'.

Alfie wouldn't move again. She knelt down and stroked his face, moving his long fuzzy mane away from his eyes. He moved to rest his chin against Hannah's cheek and nuzzled her.

'Alfie, that tickles!' Hannah said, giggling as she fell backwards on the snow once again and the rest of the carrots spilled out of her rucksack. Alfie leapt and grabbed one of the carrots, looking very cheeky as he began to munch it.

'I see what you were doing there, but you can't have all of these' Hannah said, laughing as she began to scoop them back up.

They began to head back through the trees and the snow began to fall. She knew that if she didn't get back to the stables before Ruth or her Dad came to pick her up, she could be in a lot of trouble.

As they wandered back through the forest, a loud noise caught their attention and they both stopped and turned around to look. It was the same noise Hannah had heard a few days ago, the same noise that came from the mysterious creature. The noise rumbled again through the forest, causing an avalanche of snow to fall from the trees.

Alfie began to whinny loudly and stomp his feet as the noise got nearer to them, rumbling louder and louder and creating an echo through the forest this time. Hannah scanned the area as the bushes began to rattle, closer and closer. She stepped back, preparing herself for the creature. She knew it was just inches away as the tree next to her began to shake...

Suddenly the noises stopped and the tree stopped shaking; she squinted her eyes longingly, and glanced at Alfie who looked puzzled.

There was suddenly another loud roar through the forest, causing the ground to shake and Hannah had to steady herself on the tree next to her and grip Alfie's leadrope to stop him from tumbling over. She closed her eyes as the snow began to blizzard. Struggling to see, she felt something sprint past her and she quickly tried to open her eyes, but it was too hard to battle against the blizzard of snow which was now lashing down.

\*\*\*

Hannah slowly opened her eyes. She wasn't sure how long they had been standing there but the snow had managed to cover the ground another few inches. The forest was now peaceful and there was no breeze or sound, not even from the snow which was now gently spiralling from the sky.

Alfie shook himself free of the snow which had trapped him in and Hannah did the same. They searched for the tracks of the creature once again but the snow had quickly covered them. They were just starting to head towards the oak tree when Hannah noticed a trail of golden dust... She gently crouched down and touched the dust as it shone against the snow. Alfie sniffed the snow and leapt in the air giddily.

Hannah looked at him confused; he's never been able to leap that high before she thought to herself. Alfie then got down and began to roll in the snow amongst the golden dust with his legs in the air. Hannah tutted, thinking about how cold he would get.

This time Alfie leapt high into the air, and, kicking his back feet, he got even higher. Hannah struggled to hold onto his leadrope as he jumped even further into the air. She watched, amazed, as Alfie was now flying in circles around her as she clutched the rope, not wanting to see him get any further away.

He gently landed back to the ground, and Hannah stared, amazed at what she had just witnessed. She slowly knelt down and looked at the golden dust on the ground which was brighter than anything she had ever seen. It glowed as she brushed her fingers over it and she slowly felt herself lift off the floor.

At first she panicked as she went higher into the air, but she soon settled as she began to fly around Alfie who was now on the ground below. She giggled as she once again felt the magical feeling zip through her, but it soon faded as she lowered to the ground. There was another rustle from the bushes and Hannah suddenly remembered about the creature.

'If the creature can fly then it's no wonder we can't see it' she whispered as she looked at Little Alf. The snow had once again begun to get heavier as it whirled to the ground, and Hannah knew they had to get back to the stables.

They began to move once again through the heavy snow, struggling to see as it began to blizzard again, blowing against them. It was a huge effort to battle against it as the snow was melting as it landed on Hannah and Alfie, and it was only a matter of minutes before they were both soaked. They quickly took shelter underneath one of the tall trees and huddled together out of the cold.

'We will just have to head back in the snow, Alfie' Hannah said, her teeth chattering.

Alfie was huddled next to Hannah with his feet buried in the snow and his head resting against her knee, trying to keep warm. They began to wade through the snow once again, but lifting one foot in front of the other was a huge struggle as the snow began to trap them in.

Hannah squinted, trying to see the direction back towards the stables but everything looked the same. The trees were hard to recognise as the snow began to bury their roots and cover the branches in a thick layer of snow and it soon became apparent that they were very lost...

***

The light was beginning to fade, creating new shadows and dark patches against the snow. It had finally stopped and the forest seemed peaceful, with only the rustle of the forest trees and the patter of snow as it fell from the branches. Hannah and Alfie had finally decided to take cover underneath one of the large trees as they waited for the snow to stop.

'I think the snow has stopped now Alfie. We'd best head back, I bet we will be in big trouble' Hannah sighed. Alfie snorted and leapt from underneath the tree, making a vibration as the branches shook. Hannah looked around but didn't know where they were. All the trees looked the same and there were no tracks as it was all covered in a thick layer of glistening snow.

'Which way is home, Alfie?' Hannah looked around and then glanced at Alfie to see he was looking up in the sky. She looked up to see what he was looking at. The sky was a velvet blue and the moon was just beginning to shine, but then she saw something way off in the distance... there was something moving very gracefully across the sky, she tilted her head and glanced at the object. It was moving quickly but elegantly and almost bouncing up and down. It definitely wasn't an aeroplane as it was flying too low...

Alfie whined and leapt in the air excitedly. Hannah looked at him and giggled before gazing up at the object again. It was enchanting to watch and gave Hannah a magical buzz through her body. Then she realised that following the object was a line of golden dust which shone brightly across the sky...

As the object danced, it flew in front of the moon and she saw the silhouette of Santa and his reindeers...

Hannah jumped up and down with excitement and began to wave, but she was pretty sure Santa wouldn't be able to see her, as he was high up in the sky.

'Did you see him Alfie? Did you?' Hannah squealed as Alfie bucked and reared.

### 'HO HO HO!'

Hannah looked up at the sky again to see Santa and his reindeers now flying above them, as golden dust magically swirled to the floor. Hannah, with Little Alf by her side, watched in amazement as they flew off into the night sky. There was a loud bang and a flutter of sparks and glitter as a bright star was formed in the sky. This star was brighter than any star Hannah had ever seen before and it looked bigger than the rest as it floated softly in the sky.

Alfie began to move forward in the direction of the star with his head down, dragging Hannah along behind him as he burrowed through the snow.

'Whoaaa, Alfie, slow down!' Hannah cried, as they slammed to the floor. Alfie stopped and nudged Hannah as she stood up and dusted the snow off once again.

'Alfie, it might not be that way home' Hannah said as she patted his head, but once again he began to head through the woods towards the star which was glowing fiercely in the sky, and Hannah had no option but to follow. She had no idea what time it was, but knew it was definitely past 5pm and Ruth would be back at Meadowlea Stables. She also knew her Dad would be waiting there, and wasn't looking forward to the trouble she would be in when she got back home...

The woodland echoed with every step they took through the snow, creating a boom through the trees, the rattling wind blasting through the forest, snapping the weak branches which were too heavy from the snow. Hannah jumped as they came crashing to the ground, but Alfie carried on forward, battling through the huge pile of snow, and all Hannah could do was trust that he knew the way back as the night got darker and they only appeared to be getting deeper into the forest...

***

When she heard a loud whinny and it wasn't from Little Alf, Hannah knew the stables were right in front of her.

'Well done Alfie!' she cried as she patted him and grabbed a handful of carrots from her rucksack. She had never been so happy to reach the stables. Alfie slowed down his pace, clearly tired from battling the snow, and began to munch the carrots.

As they walked up into Meadowlea Stables, Hannah looked up at the star which was still shining more brightly than the rest, and knew that was what Alfie had been following on the way home. She giggled to herself, still amazed that she had seen Santa and his reindeers. As they wandered further up the yard and towards the barn, Hannah noticed that all the lights from Ruth's house were off and the barn was quiet, with only the sound of the horses munching their hay. She looked around to see that the car park was empty and her parents were not sitting there waiting for her.

'How strange' Hannah muttered to herself as she looked at Alfie, who was yawning. She wandered down and into the barn, switching on the lights which startled some of the horses in their stables.

Once she had Little Alf tucked up in his bed she wandered up to the Meadowlea office which was joined onto Ruth's house. The notice she had seen earlier was still stuck to the door. She gently pushed open the door as snow slid down the side of it, and walked into the warm office and over to the phone.

### *2 NEW MESSAGES*

It flashed across the screen, she stood and listened to the first one. A familiar voice came across...

'Hi Ruth, its Mike, Hannah's Dad. I've tried to pick Hannah up but I can't get the car through the snow. Is it okay if she stays at yours overnight?'

### *Second message *

'Hi everyone! I'm afraid I've got stuck in the snow shopping! I won't be home tonight! Would be great if you could see to all the horses and hopefully I'll be back home in the morning'.

Hannah stared at the answering machine. Her Dad and Ruth had both got stuck in the snow, which meant nobody knew she had been missing all day...

# Chapter 6

Hannah phoned her parents and Ruth to let them know she had got their message and was still at the stables. Ruth told Hannah to make sure she locked the door and could sleep on the sofa in her house. She wandered outside to check Little Alf was okay from his journey today, and when she went into the barn she could hear the soft snores from some of the horses who were lying down in their stables. Everywhere was peaceful.

Paddy, the big chunky gyspy cob, welcomed her with a low whinny as she walked down the barn and put his head over the old wooden stable door to greet her.

'Shhhh Paddy, everyone's asleep' Hannah whispered as she stroked his face. He lifted his head up, enjoying it as Hannah scratched him underneath his chin. His breath blew warmly on her bare cheek, sending a shiver down her spine, she still hadn't managed to warm up from earlier, and the weather was turning colder as the night drew on. As Paddy breathed out she could see his breath in the icy air. His ears pricked as Hannah carried on down the barn to Alfie's stable. He let out another whinny, a little louder this time.

'Paddy! What did I say, you have to keep quiet. It's bedtime!' she whispered again as his ears twitched and he looked cheeky as he nudged her. She sneakily fed him a carrot and wandered over to Alfie's door. As she heard Paddy crunch his carrot she giggled softly, hoping he wouldn't disturb any of the other horses.

As she peered over the door she could hear the gently muffles of Alfie sleeping, he was laid up on his straw looking very hazy, not quite asleep but not fully awake, and she knew it wouldn't be long until he would be in a deep sleep. He looked so warm and cosy she just wanted to crawl in and cuddle him, but she didn't want to risk waking him up.

Hannah closed the barn door and headed up in to the yard towards Ruth's house. It had just started to snow softly again as the white flakes spiralled to the ground. As much as she loved snow she willed it to stop, otherwise her parents wouldn't be able to collect her again the next day and, as much as she loved being at Meadowlea Stables, she was starting to miss home.

It seemed very quiet around the yard with just the hoot of an owl in one of the nearby trees. She headed inside to the warmth and made herself a hot chocolate as she sat down in front of the fire, admiring Ruth's Christmas tree. It was a real one, and the needles were fresh and glossy, the golden tinsel draped over the edges, and the lights changed colour dancing up and down. The decorations were all different shapes and colours from little toy soldiers to big round baubles and the very top of the tree had a huge silver angel perched there which glittered brightly from the golden glow of the fire.

There was suddenly a low knock. Hannah turned off the TV and cautiously headed towards the door. She peered through the window but nobody was there, then she heard the low knock again and looked out towards the stables, but all she could see was the silhouetted darkness of the barn. When she heard the low knock again she realised the noise was coming from behind her and turned around to see the Christmas reef was slowly bashing against the door in the light wind.

Hannah giggled at herself. 'It's going to be a long night' she muttered as she locked the door and headed into the warmth of the room again. As the fire blazed, she was soon much warmer and thought about what she would be doing if she was at home.

It was just a few days until Christmas and usually she would be writing her Christmas letters at home with her brother John. Not wanting to break tradition, she went in search of pencils and paper, and sat down on the sofa to write her letter to Santa....

Dear Santa,

Usually I would be writing my letter in the comfort of my own home, but unfortunately this year I got trapped in the snow, so I am at Meadowlea Stables in North Yorkshire, where I keep my mini Shetland, Little Alf.

Earlier tonight I saw you flying above the mysterious forest in front of the moon. Me and Little Alf were so excited! I don't think you saw us but I did wave. It was so magic to see you flying through the air. I saw the golden dust flutter behind you. This year for Christmas I don't want to ask for a present. I know your elf's work extra hard but we have a problem at the stables.

There is a mysterious creature living in the forest and creating quite a stir. It has broken into another stable yard nearby and eaten the horse's feed. I now believe it is living in the forest, which is really bad as that means we can't ride through there with the horses. I saw some golden dust on the ground today and it made me and Alfie fly! I think this creature may be able to fly too. I was wondering if you could have a look on your sleigh?

I know it is a huge request as Christmas is getting nearer, and you will be very busy but I really would like to be able to ride again.

Love from

Hannah and Little Alf

X X

Meadowlea Stables, North Yorkshire.

After she had written the letter she gently rolled it up, wrapped a thick layer of red ribbon around it and set it next to the fire, hoping that Santa would collect it that night...

# Chapter 7

Hannah bolted upright on the sofa and saw it was still dark outside; she realised she must have fallen sleep. At first she was unsure of where she was but soon remembered the events of the previous day. A glance at the clock told her it was only 1am. As she yawned and began to pull the blanket back over her she noticed her letter to Santa had gone... She jumped off the sofa and flicked the light on, crouching down next to the fire which now had a low glow of orange as it was beginning to fade out. She could see a small pile of golden dust which was delicately balanced on the fireplace like the dust from a fairy's wings. It glittered and sparkled against the glow of the fire. She carefully moved the golden dust around with her finger and it glowed against her skin. As she moved it she noticed there was something underneath the pile...

As she gingerly swept the magical dust away she saw that there was a small pile of chocolate coins stacked on top of each other...

There was a loud bang and a whinny from one of the horses. Hannah jumped to her feet and headed

towards the window. Drawing back one of the curtains and turning the light off, she scanned the yard, but couldn't see anything...

There was another sharp bang and a clatter of things moving, and Hannah peered up at the trees, but it wasn't really windy so it couldn't be that. Then there was another whinny from one of the horses and Hannah was pretty sure it was Alfie.

She glanced at the phone, wondering whether to call her parents but she knew they wouldn't be able to get there in the snow so she scanned the yard one last time and saw the feed barn door gently swinging open. Quickly grabbing her jumper and yellow wellies which were still damp from the previous day, she scurried around to the kitchen, snatching a torch and heading outside.

The cold air instantly hit her and the soft wind numbed her face; she carefully trudged over to the feed room door, which had now swung shut. Maybe I just hadn't locked it earlier, she thought to herself as she got nearer, but she could hear the horses banging on their stable doors, clearly unsettled by something.

She creaked open the barn door, the moonlight allowing her to see just enough in front of her to walk without falling over. She tried to remember the layout of the inside of the building so she wouldn't knock anything over and disturb whatever was inside. There was untidy dusty straw leaning up against the stone wall on the right and a neat stack of sweet smelling hay behind it. Flicking the button on her torch she began to scan the area; her hands were shaking and she tried to steady them as she continued to look around the barn.

'Ahhh!' she screamed and tripped over as she saw a little mouse run in front of her. Jumping back up and rubbing her sore knee, she crept further down the barn. Holding the torch up again, she looked around. There was a small worn crack at the back of the barn which was letting through a thin layer of the moonlight which created shadows against the hay.

Then she saw something move very slowly out of the corner of her eye, and quickly turning round she shone her torch forward.

'T-WIT T-WOOO...'

Two beady eyes stared back at her.

'T-WIT T-WOO' it squawked again. She shone the torch a while longer on the barn owl in front of her before shooing it off. She knew the creature she was looking for was a lot bigger than a barn owl, and she was pretty sure they didn't eat carrots either.

After convincing herself there wasn't anything else in the feed barn, she was going to shut the door when she heard a rustle and one of the feed buckets fell over, thudding to the floor. Gently she squeaked the door open; leaving the torch off this time she crawled down to the bottom of the barn.

'Crunch, Crackle'.

She paused as she heard something eating the carrots from the feed room. It crunched them loudly and it soon became apparent it was eating more than one at a time as the loud crunches echoed around the barn.

A whinny from one of the horses stopped the creature from munching and she heard it getting nearer to her... she held her breath as the creature walked right in front of her. Struggling to see in the darkness, she could make out that the creature was tall and had four feet which banged against the stone floor.

It was almost the size of a horse, but didn't have the stocky frame of a horse, its legs seemed agile and slim but its head was larger than the rest of its body. The silhouette of the creature looked lean and maybe a little underweight, and at the front she was pretty sure it had some sort of ribbon tied around its neck. Hannah slowly reached for her torch, eager to find out what breed of animal the creature was.

As she reached for it, the creature stopped and put its nose to the floor, sniffing along the hay. Its wet nose brushed against Hannah's arms creating a tingle down her body. She tried to hold her giggles in, but accidently let one slip. The creature stopped and backed up hesitantly. Hannah kept as still as possible not wanting to scare it. She heard the creature starting to breath faster with panic but kept as still as a statue and it settled back down.

It then stepped forward again, sniffing Hannah's coat pockets and working its way up towards her face. It stopped when it reached her cheek and sniffed it curiously before licking her face, which tickled her skin. She tried not to laugh. As the moonlight caught the creature's face, she saw its big brown eyes which were soft and full of kindness - just like Alfie's. As she stood there, she tried to see past the creature's eyes, but could only see the darkness of the barn. As the creature began to sniff her pockets again it slowly began to nudge her, and wrapped its mouth around one of her pockets, trying to munch it.

'CRUNCH' she suddenly realised she must have a carrot in her pocket from having been in the forest with Alfie earlier. The creature pulled at her pocket again, knocking her to the floor. As she landed with a thud the creature stopped and took flight towards the barn door. Hannah slowly staggered up, feeling dizzy from the fall, and looked towards the barn door. There was a loud clatter of the creature's hooves as it panicked and rammed against the door, which had swung shut.

'Steady boy, it's okay' she whispered as she headed towards the door.

The creature began to ram against the door harder and harder. Hannah took a step back as she saw how strong the creature was. Now she knew she could be in great danger as she heard Alfie whinny... she knew he would be unsettled in his stable. This seemed to stop the creature... it was out of breath from trying to force the metal door open and bent over, tired and snorting from its efforts.

'It's okay, I can let you out, I promise... I won't hurt you' Hannah said calmly as she moved further forward. The creature began to snort louder, frightened by Hannah it shook its head and began to ram the door with more and more force. Scared it was going to seriously hurt itself, she knew she had to try a different tactic.

Slowly she reached down and unzipped her coat pocket, bringing out the carrot from earlier. She rolled it over the floor towards the creature. It stopped ramming against the door and slowly bent down to sniff the carrot.

'crunch...'

As it began to munch the carrot Hannah moved swiftly forward and pushed the creaking door open...

\*\*\*

There was the clatter of hooves as the creature stormed forwards, brushing Hannah with its wispy coat as it moved faster and faster out of the yard. Hannah followed, trying to get a good glimpse under the night stars.

It was moving too fast for her to keep up and leapt over the paddock fence easily. She was shocked as she had never seen something jump so elegantly before. She stopped and squinted her eyes as the creature landed swiftly and carried on moving up the field. She was pretty sure it had horns or antlers. As she saw it leap over another fence, she squinted harder and as it caught the moonlight she saw it...


The mystery creature was a reindeer...

# Chapter 8

Different questions raced through Hannah's mind. Why was there a reindeer in the North Yorkshire Dales? Was it one of Santa's reindeer? Was the reindeer hungry?

She remembered the red ribbon on the reindeer's neck and knew it must be lost from somewhere. Heading into the feed room, she switched on the light. It only gave off a small glow but it was enough for Hannah to see that the reindeer had eaten most of the horse's carrots and some of the hay...

Although a lot of the feed was gone she felt happier as she knew the reindeer wouldn't be hungry, and Ruth always kept an emergency supply in the other barn through winter in case it snowed, so the horses would have enough feed to eat if they couldn't get out through the snowy conditions.

As she slowly began to tidy up the feed room she saw  something shining in the corner. She crouched down and reached for the object, and found two tiny bells tied together on a piece of soft silky ribbon. The ribbon was bright red and laced with a silver fabric, the tiny bells were a bright gold; she gently rattled them and they jingled beautifully and echoed around the barn. She placed them in her pocket and headed in to check the horses in the stable block.

All the horses were whinnying loudly in their stables and banging against their doors. Paddy was shaking his head and pacing around his box, Ryan, the huge thoroughbred, was ramming against his door, Pepper, the other miniature Shetland, was head-butting the door and whining loudly, Hannah quickly ran down to see that Alfie had his head held high, but when he saw her he whinnied loudly and seemed to calm down.

'It's alright everyone, settle down' Hannah said soothingly as her voice echoed around the stables.

This seemed to calm most of the horses and ponies, with just a few of them left snorting on high alert. She wandered along and opened the drawer where they kept the mints for the horses, and headed down the stalls, making sure each and every one of them was okay after being unsettled by the reindeer. There was only Ryan the dapple grey who was still unsettled; all the other horses seemed to have settled down peacefully, some of them falling back to sleep again.

Lastly she headed into Alfie's stable and crouched down next to him on the soft straw, covering a yawn with her hand as she sat down. The straw on the floor rustled as Alfie moved forward next to her, blowing softly against her cheek. She held out a mint and he took it gracefully, crunching it with a grunt of great satisfaction. Alfie began to close his eyes as he rested one of his hooves and placed his chin heavily on Hannah's shoulder. She yawned again and sat back against the stable wall. It wasn't long before the pair were sleeping softly...

***

It was the kicking of Badger in the stable next to Alfie's that woke her up, and she was surprised how wide awake she felt after the previous night's events. Alfie grunted softly as she stretched her arms and legs and began to stand up. There was a dim light coming in from outside and she thought it must still be the early hours of the morning; she gently petted Alfie as she heard a loud groan from his belly.

'Alfie, you can't be that hungry!' Hannah giggled in surprise. As she unbolted the door, all the horses began to shuffle and whinny, and she heard the growl of Badger's belly too.

'You must all be starving by the sound of it!'

All the horses whinnied and began kicking their stable doors.

'I better get you fed then' she said, smiling as she went down each stable, filling up the hay nets with the dusty hay and sugary haylege. She also filled up each horse's food bowl with pony nuts and apples, and each bowl with water, then began to muck each stable out.

By the time she had finished she was exhausted, and slowly opening the barn door she could see that the light was beginning to fade again.

'That's odd' Hannah thought to herself as she wandered up to the house. When she opened the door she glanced at the wooden clock.

6:00 pm

She glanced at the clock again, uncertain as to what she had just read.

6:01pm

If it was past 6:00pm that means she must have been asleep all day! Running through to check the phone she found...

## *1 NEW MESSAGE*

'Hi Hannah, please ring me back as soon as you get this. Looks like we're still stuck in the snow and can't get up there'.

She played the message again and heard Ruth's voice even clearer this time, she couldn't believe she had managed to sleep for one whole day! No wonder the horses were hungry. That also meant it was only four days until Christmas!

Hannah got an excited little buzz through her body as she phoned Ruth to let her know she and the horses were all okay.

***

The night soon became dark, but the stars shone brightly. Hannah stood outside wrapped up in her thick coat, woolly hat and the red scarf and matching mittens her Mum had knitted her. She had borrowed a spare pair of snow boots from the tack room and trudged out into the cold with a steaming hot chocolate. She wasn't too happy about having to stay the night by herself at the stables again, but having the horses nearby was a comfort. She lingered outside the stable, looking into the sky for the star she had seen a few nights ago, but they all looked the same, and a million miles away. Pulling the creaky barn door open to do a final check on the horses, she heard a jingle of bells...

As she scanned the sky it all looked quiet and peaceful, but then she heard the bells again. Looking up and around in the sky, it all looked the same with just the stars twinkling, but this time she heard the bells jingling more rapidly and getting nearer and nearer, and as she tilted her head back she saw the cantering hooves of reindeers flying above her, the jingling bells were strapped to their brown harness, which was pulling a large wooden red sleigh, and she heard the bellow of Santa once again.

'HO HO HO!'

The bells jingled in rhythm through the air, the sleigh shone a beautiful red and the reindeers were polished and pulling forward strongly as golden dust swirled around them.

Hannah stood there amazed as she watched them glide through the air gracefully, and begin to swirl around the forest, getting lower and lower... at first Hannah thought they were falling and held her breath in panic, but then realised they were searching for something...

'He must have got my letter!' she shouted as she watched his sleigh gently lower into the forest...

# Chapter 9

Once again Hannah and Alfie were battling through the snow and heading towards the forest, but this time there was a huge golden glow surrounding it, making it easy to see exactly where they were going. As they came closer to the outside of the trees, the forest was closely knitted together with golden dust, making it impossible to enter. Alfie pulled to the left, pulling Hannah behind him. She ran next to him through the snow; trying to keep up he suddenly stopped...

They turned to the forest and saw there was a tiny gap which hadn't been knitted together with the golden dust, and Alfie slowly moved forward... and then vanished...

'Alfie, Alfie' she whispered. Worriedly she got down on her knees and tried to crawl through the gap, but it was as if something was pulling her back and trying to keep her out of the forest. Whatever she tried, she couldn't enter... Standing up again, she suddenly had an idea...

'Believe in magic and you will find it'

As she whispered the words, a huge archway began to form, sparks and dust flying off in all directions, making a curved opening into the forest. She saw Alfie standing on the other side, waiting.

*'What took you so long?'*

Hannah stared at Alfie as a huge smile spread across her face

'Alfie, you're back!' she cried as she dropped to her knees and gave him a huge cuddle. Alfie nuzzled her.

*'Quick. We have to go, the magic is fading...*
*Santa won't be here much longer'*

Hannah looked at the golden dust surrounding the forest and realised Alfie was right - it was now beginning to fade. They began to run towards the centre of the forest where the glow was shining strongly; they could feel the magic fading behind them and turning into the dark night which forced them to go faster, and, as they got nearer, Hannah could see the reindeers and Santa's sleigh...

She approached slowly and calmly with Alfie next to her, not wanting to startle the reindeers, but they were already looking ahead and didn't seem phased by her arrival.

The reindeers jingled their bells and Alfie swished his head in excitement as they stamped their feet. Hannah giggled, which made the reindeers more excited and ringing their bells even louder.

### 'WELL - what do we have here?'

Whipping around she was met by two large polished black boots. She slowly moved her eyes up to see Santa's glistening red suit and his jolly face staring down at her. She gulped, amazed but not sure what to say.

### 'Hannah and Alfie, I believe!'

He bellowed out.

Alfie shook his head and jumped off all four feet, bucking and rearing, clearly excited. 'Yes that's us!' Hannah said, giddily.

'Well Hannah and Alfie, I got your letter about a strange creature roaming in the forest, and it sounded like one of my young reindeers, Mistletoe. I was out training him the other day ready for Christmas Eve when we were hit by a terrible snowstorm which forced us to land just down the road in a small village called Leyburn. A huge blizzard came and poor Mistletoe got unattached from the sleigh and ran off. I haven't been able to find him since, but when I got your letter it gave me hope that maybe he was around here somewhere'

'We've seen him! Just a few days ago he broke into Meadowlea Stables feed barn and ate all of our carrots, but I scared him and he came running into the forest!' Hannah cried.

'Well that is really interesting... I have searched ☆ everywhere for him after getting your letter, but, since Mistletoe is only a young reindeer, we teach them back at the North Pole to come back to the bells on the sleigh. Every reindeer has a bell attached around their neck so if they get lost it reminds them to go back to the same bell. I fear poor Mistletoe must have lost his bell, and that's why we can't find him' ☆

Hannah looked at Santa worriedly, fearing they may never find Mistletoe again, when Alfie nudged her coat pocket and it suddenly began to jingle.

'He has lost his bell! I found this next to the feed barn' Hannah shouted as she pulled the bell out of her pocket and shook it...

The reindeers began to jingle the bells on the sleigh and Santa started to laugh happily.

### 'Good Work Alfie!'

Santa said as he gave Alfie a carrot to munch.

**'Well, what are you waiting for? Ring the bell! Let's get Mistletoe home!'**

'Will it work if I do it?' Hannah asked, hesitantly.

**'Of course! You believe in magic don't you?'**

'I certainly do!' she beamed, looking at Alfie. She slowly stepped forward, clutching onto Little Alf's leadrope, closed her eyes, and rang the bell...

There was the rustle of the nearby trees and a loud roaring sound through the forest, the same noise they had heard previously. She heard the jingle of the other reindeer bells and she knew that Mistletoe was in front of her… she gingerly opened her eyes to see him emerging from the trees…

He was much smaller than the other reindeers and still had large fluffy patches where his baby hair was. The reindeers all grunted happily and jingled their bells as Mistletoe approached. As soon as he spotted Santa and the reindeers he began to bound towards them.

'Good to have you back, Mistletoe!'

Santa boomed across the forest.

Hannah stood amazed as the bell glowed in her hand, creating a swirl of dust and sending a magical buzz through her again.

'May I?'

Santa asked as he outstretched his hand towards Hannah. She handed him the bell and he clipped it on to Mistletoe's red ribbon at the front of his neck. It sparkled and gleamed, making a huge glow of golden dust around him, and in a matter of seconds the dirt and wispy bits of hair had vanished from his coat and he had been transformed into a gleaming reindeer with a coat which shone as brightly as the others, and he was now harnessed to the front of the sleigh.

'Wow' Hannah whispered as she stared at him.

**'Well, I'd best be on my way back home, lots of preparing to do before Christmas Eve! And Mrs Claus will be wondering where I've got to'**

'I bet there is a lot to do!' Hannah giggled.

**'There certainly is! You'd better hop in both of you, and I'll take you back to the stables'**

'Really!' Hannah beamed, as Alfie jumped in the air. Hannah stepped into the back of Santa's sleigh. It was much bigger once you got inside it!

'I always wondered how you managed to fit all the presents in here!' Hannah chuckled as Alfie stepped in.

**'HOLD ON TIGHT!'**

A loud bang sent them flying into the air, and Hannah clutched the side of the sleigh giddily as they flew high in the night sky.

## 'Come on Mistletoe pull forward'

They landed swiftly outside the stable barn, the bells jingling as Hannah stepped off the sleigh with Alfie.

**'Well Thank you for all your hard work, both of you. I couldn't have done it without you!'**

Hannah giggled and Alfie whinnied loudly.

'Right I'd better be going! Lots to do before Christmas Eve and the reindeers need their rest before the big night...'

Hannah stood with Alfie on the ground below as they watched Santa fly gracefully into the sky. He swirled around Meadowlea Stables waving, and she could faintly hear the sound of the reindeer bells as they got further away and, with a blast of golden dust, they shot into the bright star...

They stared at the sky for a while longer admiring the star, and then Hannah went to put Alfie in his stable for the night...

***

The next few days passed with a buzz. The snow eventually stopped and Ruth and her parents managed to dig through the snow and make it up to the stables.

Hannah was very pleased to be able to go
back home and have the comfort of her
warm bed. Sleeping on the stable floor had
caused her to have a sore back, and
suddenly she was hit with the Christmas
rush, helping her Mum prepare the Christmas dinner
on Christmas eve and finishing the final decorations
outside with her Dad.

Every night Hannah looked up into the sky after
feeding Alfie and could still see the star shining
brightly, but she still wondered if it had all just been
a dream...

It was the night before Christmas Eve and
Hannah was exhausted from the past few
days... she opened door **24** on her advent
calendar and headed into her warm bed,
hanging up her red stocking on the fire place
as she went...

# Chapter 10

Hannah woke up the next day with a twinkly feeling in her stomach. Had the last few days all been a dream? She glanced at her clock - 6:30am. Still too early to wake anyone up. She quietly crept downstairs to see the gifts glittering under the tree lights. She was so excited and couldn't wait for her parents to wake up. She turned around and was heading back upstairs when she kicked something small and looked down to see a tiny gift wrapped up delicately with a huge red ribbon around it... Carefully she turned the tag over, as golden dust fluttered to the ground...

*To Hannah & Alfie*

*Thank you for all the help over the past week!*

*Love Santa, the reindeers and Mistletoe*

*Xx*

Hannah read the tag once again.

It wasn't a dream, she really had been on the adventure a few days ago! She slowly crept back upstairs to her bedroom; the light was just beginning to shine through the curtains as she sat on her bed looking at the parcel. She gingerly untied the red ribbon and carefully took off the silver paper, and in front of her was the most beautiful present she had ever seen.

Shaking it up and down, the snow began to glitter, and inside the globe was a statue of Hannah, Little Alf and Mistletoe...

MERRY CHRISTMAS!

X

**★★★★**

We hope everyone enjoyed another one of Little Alf's Magical Adventures...!

This is a special addition to the other Little Alf Adventure books.

Hannah Russell, Little Alf's owner, started 'The Magical Adventures of Little Alf' series in 2014.

The first two books in the series are:

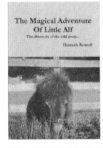

Book 1 - The Magical Adventure of Little Alf - The discovery of the wild pony

Book 2 - The Magical Adventure of Little Alf - The Enchanted Forest

The next book in the series is due to be published in 2016!

All the books can be purchased online at:

www.littlealf.com

## Little Alf photo Gallery!

Training with Hannah 'Kiss'

Running through the Paddock at Meadowlea Stables.

# Rugged up in winter!

# Playing in the snow!

## About the Author

Hannah Russell is the proud owner of Little Alf who lives behind her house in the North Yorkshire Dales alongside her other horses, dogs and guinea pigs!

Hannah published her first book in 2014 at the young age of 17. 'The Magical Adventure of Little Alf – The discovery of the wild pony' was the first book in the Little Alf series. After publishing her first book, she decided to design a clothing range exclusive to Little Alf. This has now expanded into a wide variety of children, adult and baby clothing. This can also be found at:

www.littlealf.com

In 2015 Hannah published her second book in the series 'The Magical Adventure of Little Alf –The enchanted forest'

Now...

'Little Alf the Magic helper'

...has been added as a sequel to the collection. Hannah loves Christmas and thought it would be a very good special addition!

In the next few months Hannah will be bringing out her third book in the series. This is due to be launched at the start of 2016!

As well as writing the Little Alf series, Hannah has now started to write books aimed at teenagers which are planned for publishing in summer 2015. 'The Travel Girl' is the first in the series. Hannah plans to publish more books over the next few years.

Through their books Hannah and Little Alf help support the Riding for the Disabled Association, for whom she is an active volunteer at her local RDA centre. Sometimes she takes Little Alf along too!

Since publishing the very first book in 2014, Hannah and Little Alf have begun to do book signing tours where you can meet them in person and get your books signed! Also, since Hannah does a lot of training with horses, you may also find her with Little Alf at agricultural shows, taking part in main ring performances! If you keep a lookout on their website and follow their blog you will be able to find out which destination they are heading to next!

You can also tweet Hannah and ask her questions on her Twitter account at:

@hannahrussell26

Or @AlfLittle


# Hannah & Little Alf

x

Printed in Great Britain
by Amazon